The Legend of the Three Brothers

Written by
Jill Atkins

Illustrated by
Jim Atherton

Long ago, there lived an old king who had three sons: Lech ('*Leck*'), Czech ('*Check*') and Rus ('*Roos*').

One day, the king grew gravely ill. He sent for his sons.

"When I am gone," he whispered, "I want you to promise to share my lands between you and to live together in peace."

The three brothers bowed their heads.

"We promise, Father," they said.

The very next day the king died. The brothers were sad, but they remembered what their father had said to them.

They shared the land fairly between them and they built homes for their families and friends.

However, as time went by, their families grew larger and they all needed more space.

"Let's travel and search for new lands," said Lech. "We need to find enough space for our families to live in comfort."

The three families packed warm clothes, tents to sleep in and food for the journey. Then Lech, Czech and Rus mounted their horses and set off. They rode side-by-side and their families travelled behind them in wagons.

They rode for many weeks, over high mountains, over wide rivers, through thick forests and across vast areas of wild country.

At last, they reached a deep valley surrounded by seven hills. Lech led everyone up one of the hills.

There, on the top of the hill, stood a giant oak tree. Flying above the oak tree they could see a great white eagle. It swooped in large circles above the tree.

Lech lifted his hands towards the eagle.

"This is a sign from the gods," he cried. "Let's stop a while and look around."

Climbing the tree, he stared all around him.

He could see for miles in every direction: an enormous lake and thick dark forest lay nearby, green hills lay to the south and endless flat plains spread out to the east.

When he climbed down, he told Rus and Czech what he had seen.

"I like the endless flat plains," said Rus, pointing to the east. "We could grow good crops there and become rich. I would like to go that way."

"I prefer the green hills of the south," said Czech. "We could keep animals there to graze on the grass. That's a better way of life for us."

Lech said nothing. He was watching the eagle as it swooped down to its nest in the oak tree.

Then he stared in wonder as the eagle spread its wings and soared again, high into the evening sky.

As it rose, a ray of light from the setting sun shone on its wings. The body and head of the eagle stayed pure white, but the wings were suddenly tipped with gold.

Lech climbed onto a fallen tree trunk.

"Czech, Rus, everyone!" he called. "Listen to me."

Everyone gathered round.

"You all saw the eagle," he cried. "It was telling us that this is a special place. So here is where we will stay. This will be our new home!"

But Rus spoke to his people and asked them which way they would like to go.

"With you, to the plains in the east!" they shouted.

Czech hurried away and asked his people where they wanted to go.

"With you, to the green hills in the south," they yelled.

Lech turned to his people.

"Where would you like to settle?" he asked.

"Here!" they cried. "Like you, we've seen the eagle. We understand the sign. We wish to stay here."

Lech called his brothers back.

"We have no need to argue," he said, "and Father wanted us to live in peace."

"We'll each go our own way," said Czech.

"And we'll still remain friends," said Rus.

That night, they all had a great feast.

The next morning, the three brothers hugged each other and said farewell.

Rus and his followers went east to settle on the plains. Their country was named Russia.

Czech and his followers went south to the green hills of their country that we now call the Czech Republic.

When Czech and Rus had gone, Lech spoke to his people again.

"We shall call this place Gniezno ('G-*nee-ez-no*')," he declared, "because that means 'eagle's nest'."

Straight away, Lech and his people set to work.

They built a large town on the seven hills. It took them many years.

At last, when the town was finished, Lech stood back and smiled.

"We need a flag," he declared. "It will have a white eagle with spread wings, on a red background."

His people agreed. "We remember the sign," they said. "It was the eagle that helped us choose this place."

Soon the flag flew over the town of Gniezno.

Gniezno became the first capital city of the country we now call Poland.

And that is the story of how Poland began!